An adoption story does not start when the family brings a child into their home. Rather, it begins long before that, as it starts as soon as the Birth Mother makes an ever so careful, loving decision to put her child's needs ahead of her own heart and desires. During the adoption planning process, a Birth Mother (the Hopeful Mother) is encouraged to select a name for her son or daughter, even though this will not often be the name that the Adoptive Parents (the Chosen Parents) select. In naming her child, it connects the Birth Mother to her beloved child forever in her heart. This name is a name that is still her own when her child takes on the name of another family. The Adoptive Family also carefully selects a name for their new child, which is a name that holds special meaning to them as a family and to their new precious gift.

Chelsey has so eloquently captured both Mothers' stories, with one child that connects two unique families in life forever. This story demonstrates both the extraordinary struggle of a Birth (Hopeful) Mother and the selfless love she puts into her decision, as well as the nervousness, excitement, and love that the Adoptive (Chosen) Family has in preparation for their new little loved one. One child has been so loved by two families that he or she is given two very special names: one from his Birth Mother, and one from his Adoptive Family, both loving this child for the rest of their lives.

I would like to extend a kind thank you to my amazing friends
and family who encouraged and celebrated with me during this
journey! To my awesome children who asked many questions, supported
and cheered me on through the process, thank you and I love
you dearly! For my sweet husband who worked tirelessly, staying
up late nights and putting his own projects on hold to partner with me
on this book to bring my vision to life; thank you for always helping
me chase my dreams! I love you!

Chelsey

This is a beautiful story of adoption written by Chelsey Simmons.
There is nothing better in this world than knowing you are loved.
Chelsey is the most loving, giving, and beautiful person I
have ever met. Her abundant blessings and love that
she pours out on others is the very reason she was able to convince
me that the adopted child in this book was loved by everyone.
It was such a blessing for me to read this because it reminded
me of how much I love my son who I adopted and how much
love the birth mother showed by blessing me with my child.
I know this book will warm your heart as it has mine.

Viola Echols, Author

This is a story about Open Adoption. It is about love, bravery, patience, strength, worry, sadness, fear, healing and hope.

For my sweet J.E.B. and for my beautiful B.M.B. who is stronger and braver than anyone I know.

ISBN 9781731309051

a story about open adoption

the boy with
two names

Written by: Chelsey Blackketter Simmons

Illustrated by: Curtis Simmons & Chelsey Blackketter Simmons

There once was a boy who was
so loved that when he was born,
he was given two names.

While he grew strong and healthy
in his hopeful mother's belly,
he was loved.

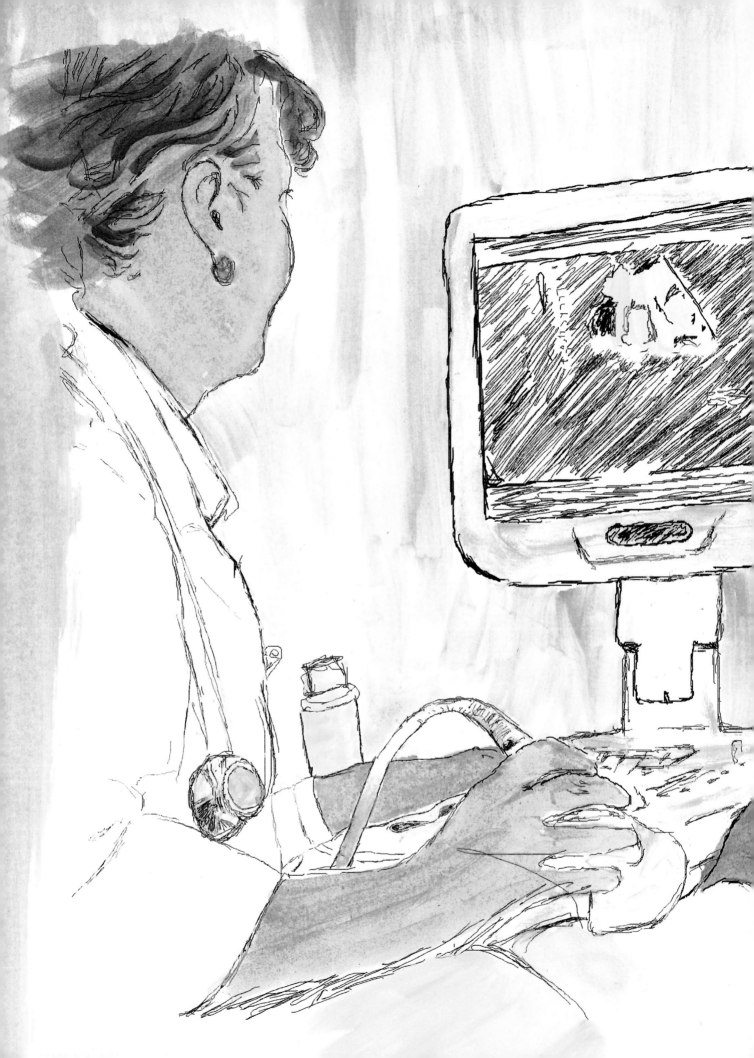

At every doctor's appointment, sonogram, and check-up, he was loved.

Even though she wanted
nothing more than to
cherish him forever, she
made the choice to
find him the
perfect family,
and as she spent hours
looking through the
family albums,
he was loved.

When the hopeful mother knew in her heart this was the one, and she met the chosen mother, he was loved.

As the chosen mother and
father prepared a room
with anxious excitement,
he was loved.

When it was finally time for
the boy with two names to be
born and both mothers
drove to the hospital,
he was loved.

As the hopeful mother struggled through a long day preparing to bring him into the world, he was loved.

When he met
his big and
unique family,
he was loved.

The first time his hopeful mother held him close and kissed his sweet cheeks, he was loved.

As the hopeful mother stared
into his big brown eyes and chose
a name for him that she would
keep forever in her heart,
he was loved.

The first time his hopeful mother
placed him in the arms
of his chosen mother,
he was loved.

While the hopeful mother sat
with empty arms and tears
streaming down her face,
he was loved.

As the chosen
parents
packed their
precious son
in his car seat
for the drive
home,
he was loved.

As the weeks passed by and the
chosen parents hugged,
cuddled and nurtured him,
he was loved.

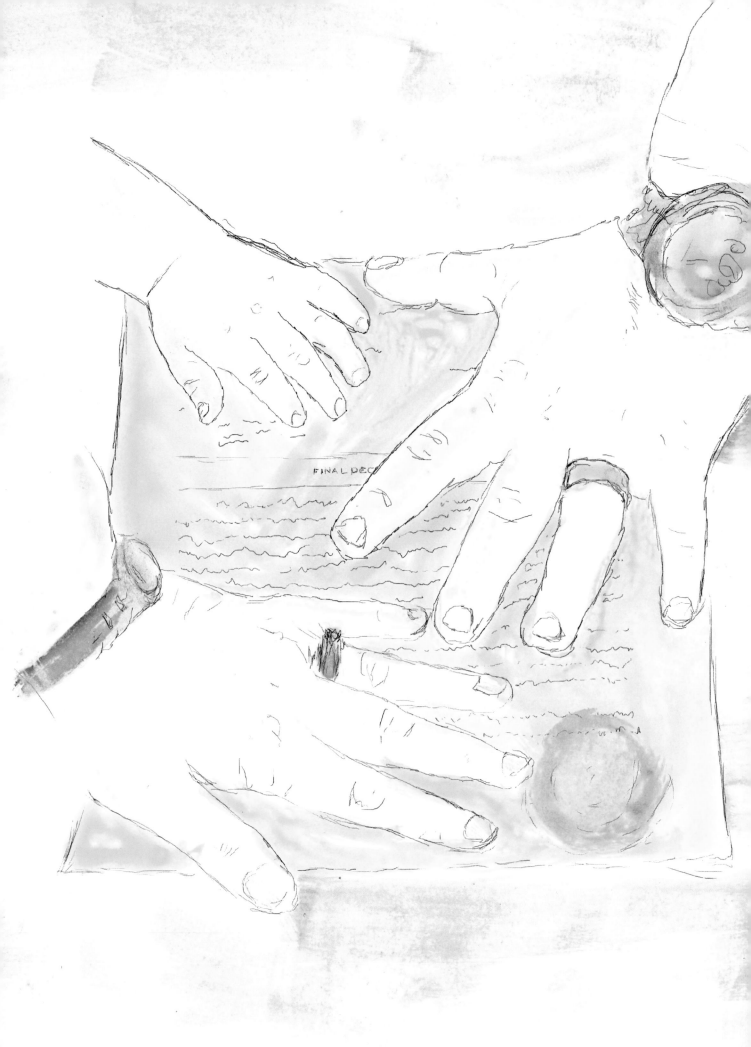

When the chosen parents met
the judge on the big day and
chose a name for him to
carry through his life,
he was loved.

As the years went by and
milestones were met,
he was loved.

While the hopeful mother watched from afar as he grew into a man, he was loved.

Then one day, he explained to his own children that even though his story began unexpectedly, from beginning to end he was so loved that he was given two names.

Made in the USA
Middletown, DE
24 January 2019